ISBN: 978-1-953697-10-3 (Paperback)
ISBN: 978-1-953697-11-0 (Hardcover)
ISBN: 978-1-953697-12-7 (Ebook)

Library of Congress Control Number: 2021918386
Any references to historical events, real people, or real places are used fictitiously. Names, characters, and places are products of the author's imagination.

Written by Rikkianisha Hunt.
Illustrated by Maria Russo.

Printed by Amazon and IngramSpark in the United States of America.

First printing edition 2022.

Asante Publishing, LLC
2628 Abbott Road SW
Conyers, Georgia, 30094

www.asantepublishing.com

FRANKIE
FOUR EYES
&
ZINDI ZIMA

Written by Rikkianisha Hunt
Illustrated by María Octavia Russo

For Anthony Jordan Hunt,
the most awesome nephew ever!

Today was a special day. Frankie's class was going on a field trip to the Zoo of Kazoo.

The Zoo of Kazoo was known far and wide for its world-famous animals.

The peacocks had the most beautiful, colorful feathers anyone had ever seen.

The giraffes had
the longest necks.

The crocodiles had the sharpest, shiniest teeth.

Everyone loved the zebras;
they were the main attraction.

The zebras at the Zoo of Kazoo had the most amazing, bold stripes.

Frankie could barely hold in his excitement!
He couldn't wait to see the animals.

If only he could see…

Frankie was the only kid in his class that wore glasses, and he was ashamed to wear them.

Frankie's mom was always telling him that they set him apart and made him unique. He didn't want to be unique.

He was afraid someone would make fun of him or call him names, like Frankie Four Eyes.

So, he kept them in his backpack.

Without his glasses, the field trip was not so fun.
The peacocks were a blur of colors.

The giraffes were long blobs.

The crocodiles looked like green logs.

When they reached the zebras, the zookeeper made an announcement. A baby zebra had been born that morning, a girl.

Frankie was not about to miss this. He shyly pulled out his glasses, put them on and joined his classmates. Everyone tried to get a look at the baby zebra.

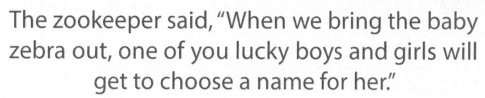

The zookeeper said, "When we bring the baby zebra out, one of you lucky boys and girls will get to choose a name for her."

Everyone raised their hands and shouted, "ME, ME, PICK ME!"

The zookeeper looked at the group and pointed right at Frankie.

"How about the young man in the glasses?"
"Would you like to name her?"

Frankie could feel everyone staring at him…and his glasses.

But he wasn't going to pass up this special chance to name the new zebra!

As they brought her out, a hush fell over the group.

From her nose to her toes, she was unique. There was something quite different about her. She was special.

She didn't have stripes, she had spots!

A special zebra deserved a special name. Frankie stood in front of everyone and said, "I want to name her Zindi Zima".

The crowd began to clap and cheer, "Hooray for Zindi Zima, the spotted zebra!"

As Frankie made his way back to the group, everyone told him what a good job he had done. Frankie was so happy, he forgot he had his glasses on.

Until Lauren Abigail pointed right at them. She said, "Nice glasses".

Frankie smiled, pushed his glasses up on his nose and said, "Thanks".

He liked being unique.

Fun facts:
A baby zebra is called a foal.
A group of zebras is called a dazzle.
A real spotted zebra was born in Kenya in 2019.
It takes a whole year for a baby zebra to be born.
A zebra is black with white stripes.

About the Author

RIKKIANISHA HUNT is as agile in literature as she is in life; turning her talents to any genre, and her mind to any challenge. Owner and author at Asante Publishing, LLC, Rikkianisha is a Maternal-Newborn nurse by day, a non-profit entrepreneur—also by day—and mother to Mason (mostly by day, but quite often by night, too). In the spaces between, she can be found crafting heart-warming stories in her home office on the outskirts of Atlanta, Georgia. It's thanks to her mini-me assistant that she's earned a place in her little reader's big hearts, as Mason gives endless inspiration for her children's books. Together, they make their days by creating chaos in the kitchen, finding peace out in nature, and growing their collection of Lego empires.

Made in the USA
Columbia, SC
09 August 2022